CW00864695

The Bully Space Force to the Rescue

Carolyn Spencer

AuthorHouse™
1663 Liberty Drive
Bloomington, IN 47403
www.authorhouse.com
Phone: 1 (800) 839-8640

This book is printed on acid-free paper.

ISBN: 978-1-7283-4979-4 (sc)
978-1-7283-4977-0 (hc)
978-1-7283-4978-7 (e)

Library of Congress Control Number: 2020904429

Print information available on the last page.

Published by AuthorHouse 03/12/2020

authorHOUSE®

Author: **Carolyn Spencer**

Illustrator: **Clarissa David**

Dedicated to my parents, Doris and Richard Royer

Special thanks goes to my son,
David William Spencer,
for his creative inspiration.

Setting: The Thorny Thicket Woodlands by the bay, not far from Foxaloon Woodlands Elementary.

Characters: Wolverina, Foxanna, Bully Space Force (Smarty Pantaloons, Lord Computesalot, Lord Cyborgeon Bonaparte, Lord Cyperdione), Superintendent Wendell Wolfson, Cool Granddaddy Big Dwayne, Mr. Snarl the wonderful assistant.

Introduction

School is not in session at this time. The principals Wolverina and Foxanna (along with their staff and other principals) are headed to a wonderful working and relaxing "Principal Outdoor Autumn Retreat Convention Picnic".

Principals Wolverina Woollyclaws and Foxanna Powerpaws were headed onto two party buses. Each of these was driven by their own robotic computers, Senor Smarty Pantaloons and Lord Cyborgeon Bonaparte, along with other principals and Superintendent Wendell Wolfson. Wendell Wolfson wanted to relax as he had just had an important meeting with all the principals the past week. He told the principals that certain teachers were to be closely monitored and brought to his office ASAP. They were all traveling to Cape Outspace near the point on the sandy seaside, which was nestled deep into the notoriously thorny thickets of the lush, yet bushy woodlands. It was just at the beginning of autumn when the new school session year was about to begin. They yearned to discuss exciting educational ideas and enjoy fascinating food and games while preparing for the new school year ahead!

STOP

Wolverina and Foxanna did not know that Lord Cyborgeon Bonaparte had been previously receiving information. Lord Cyborgeon was a member of The Bully Space Force on planet Bullytron, located east of planet Aurora Bullyalis. The information he had been receiving from Senor Smarty Pantaloons was about the bullying behaviors of Wolverina and Foxanna, the two principals. Lord Cyborgeon was anxious to observe the behaviors of the principals near the thorny woodland thickets on this clear, but windy fall day. The smell of pumpkin in the vines was deliciously all around them. Wolverina and Foxanna were anxious to have a fun and exciting time. Little did they know that their own personal robotic computers, members of The Bully Space Force, were monitoring them on BWWW.com. This was known to few as "The Bully World Wide Web", an intergalactic space force observatory located between the galaxies Snika, Mika, and the loadstar, Bullika.

Deep into the wilderness of wild flowers, margarineflies, pumpkins, gourds and bullygoats, no one knew that the notorious bully spider monsters were thrashing about. They were just waiting to attack if need be. The fearsome monsters were sharpening and greasing up their thorns as they so cautiously monitored the actions of Wolverina and Foxanna. They had been supplied with personal outernet computers brought to them by Lord Cyborgeon and Senor Smarty Pantaloons. The bully spider monsters were housed on the thorny, hallowed-out trees by the windy wild waves near the seaside. They had sprung with leaps from the high water and hid before the picnic day to be ready for bullies. Oh, how they had trained and waited for this important day. Their special mission was to save the Wolverton Woods from mean, hateful bullies once and for all and forever!

Wolverina had attended the "Bully-No-More" workshop over the summer break so she could try and help her students to be better to one another and also to work on her own self-improvement problems. If she felt an urge to bully coming her way then she knew what she had to do! She was ready to try to stop her bullying ways! In her own heart, she felt as if a change had taken place. She was trying with all her might to finally be free from her old tactics of ridiculing, mocking, and bullying others.

Principal Foxanna, however, had not desired to attend the "Bully-No-More" workshop. She had decided to go on a fabulous summer luxury cruise to Bamaica where there were beautiful turquoise waters and lofty hillsides that grew her precious coffee beans. Those coffee beans were meant to produce enough caffeine to make what she called her "Bully Brew" which she needed morning, noon, and night to plan her agenda.

Cruise

The principals began setting up the picnic tables with their homemade goodies. Wolverina brought her famous "pomegranate pudding". Foxanna brought coffee cake made with her specialty Bamaican coffee brought back from her recent relaxing luxury vacation. The other educators and principals also put their goodies out to share. Being such a balmy, sunny, colorful day, all seemed well and almost like Utopia in the thorny thicket woodlands near the windy seaside - but action was about to begin! The Bully Space Force was recording and monitoring everything!

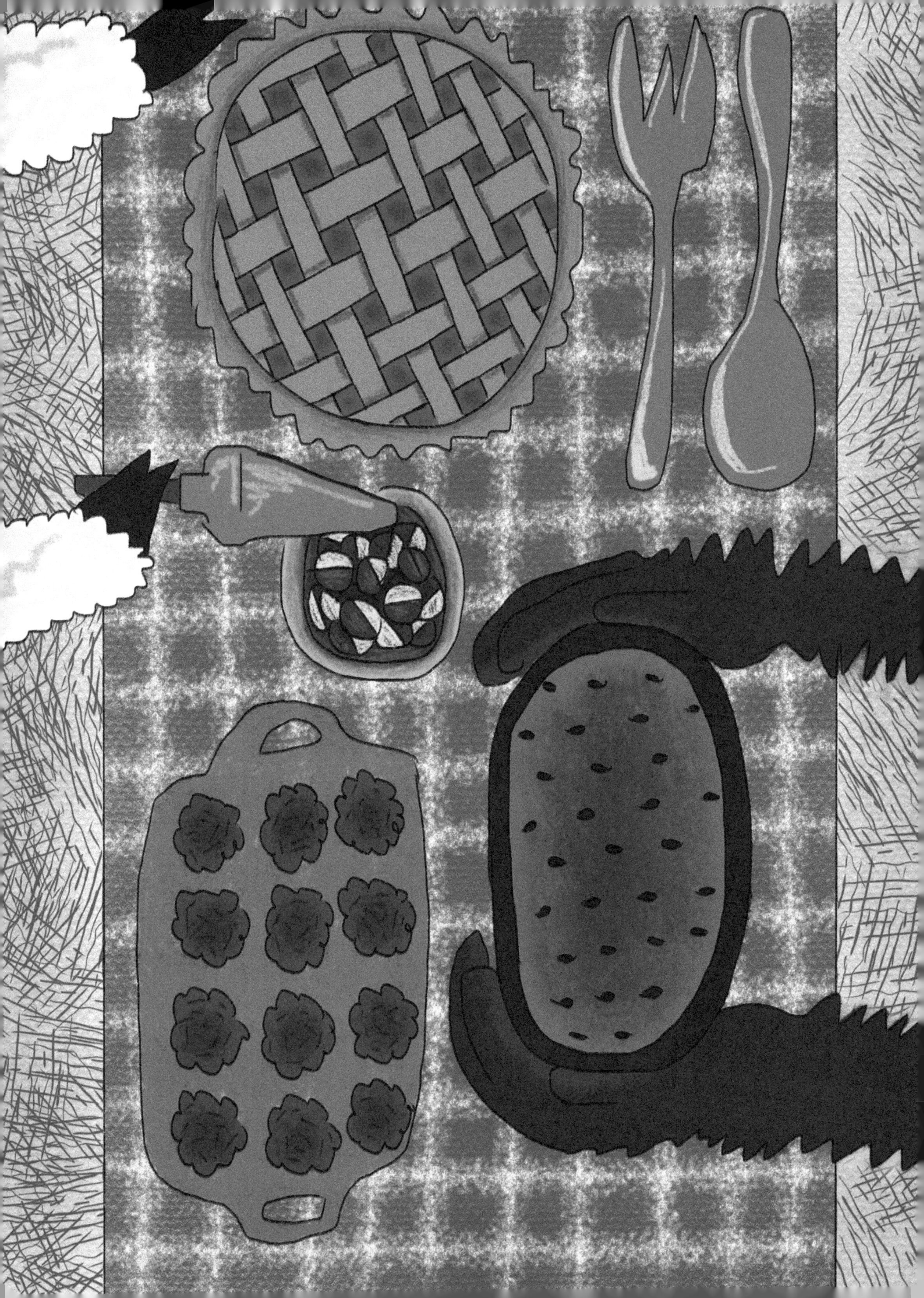

Superintendent Wendell Wolfson had set up the bully goat stakes for the bully shoe game. Cool Granddaddy Big Dwayne was setting up the woollyball nets in the gritty sand. Wendell was adamant about the principals and his staff getting their exercise. He knew that after their hearty breakfasts and lunches and stuffing their chubby cheeks that they would all need to burn off this blubber.

Meanwhile, the principals and staff members of Wolverton Woods and Foxaloon Elementary Schools were eating heartily. The menu consisted of fried dogfish, angel eggs, Scotch fries, cold dogs, and yamburgers on the flaming grill. Mr. Snarl, Foxanna's trustworthy assistant, was flipping the so-called delights high in the sky. Mouths were watering and waiting for seconds and thirds. The food was delicious, delectable and delightful. It was nothing like their school's lunchroom was noted for.

KiSS
the
CHEF

Foxanna's and Wolverina's bully bellies were full. The other staff members had also filled up. Now the games began! Foxanna and Wolverina started pitching the goat shoes. Wolverina had a slight edge over Foxanna and her goat shoes seemed to be just gliding toward the stakes, whereas Foxanna's would go to the right or the left or not quite make the mark. Foxanna blurted out, "Your hairy arms make them glide easier in the air." She seemed to be on a caffeine high from all the Bamaican coffee she kept sipping. Her vicious words continued to insult Wolverina. As Wolverina began to pitch, Foxanna purposely put her foot out to trip her. The pitch went haywire and everyone nearby had to duck. "Watch out," Mr. Snarl yelled, "she is trying to trip you!"

The tall Foxaloon water tower, a landmark, was hovering over the woodlands picnic area. The little bully spider monsters had been notoriously taking information and relaying it to Lord Computesalot. They were disguised for they blended in well with the vibrant fall colors. As they jumped from the water tower to observe and relay information, no one sensed their activity! Yes, the woodlands were full of creatures so nobody suspected, since they were small and quick, that they were secretly monitoring bully activity. They had been building a code-web for the universal, outer space Bully Worldweb - a web so strong that it could never be destroyed! It seemed that their giant fly, Foxanna, was about to be entrapped and sent away to be deprogrammed from a big bully to a more caring, compassionate, and kinder principal Foxanna. The Bully Space Force did not have time to waste!

Before the games and activities resumed, Wendell Wolfson called everyone over to the tent for dessert time and a brief talk about the upcoming year. The prickly bully monsters had been making observations and were sharpening up their pricklies. Lord Cyborgeon received information from Lord Computesalot who had been monitoring the events along with Smarty Pantaloons. They cautiously texted back and forth through high speed outernet.

Now the volleyball games were beginning! Tummies were full and hanging down from the heaviness of the food that had settled there. The ball flew over the net-back and forth-until it was to the advantage point percent of Wolverina. Foxanna screamed out, "You ate like a pig-more than anyone else! How can you possibly get that ball over the net?" The bully monsters were turning colors like fall leaves, from bright orange to vivid red. All the while, Planet Bullytron and its ruler Lord Computesalot from Bully Space Force were preparing for a new visitor! "Bullying must be stopped. Enough is enough!" they declared.

The staff was now ready to relax by the seaside and enjoy the beautiful sun setting over the incoming waves and colorful hillsides before returning home. Smarty Pantaloons and Lord Cyborgeon started up the buses and Mr. Snarl loaded them up for the trip back. Wolverina, all the while, was feeling the effects of the bullying and was not well. She felt badly about herself and very sad!

Foxanna had left her purse on one of the picnic tables deep in the Woodlands. She realized this when she was home. In her proud and haughty way though, she did not want to admit to anyone how forgetful she sometimes was, so she secretly planned to drive back there by herself to retrieve it as soon as possible. It was a beautiful drive, and the next day she could use the long ride to relax and plan while singing in the car and slurping Bamaican coffee from her "Foxy Lady" mug.

FOXY

Upon arriving, Foxanna parked her car in the parking lot and she began boldly trotting down the lined parkway to the spot where she had left her purse. As she walked along singing, the prickly little bully monsters were keeping an ever so watchful eye on her. Little did she know that Lord Computesalot had programmed them with ultrasonic devices that were capable of lifting her to the outer realms of the Cosmic Bullytron Orbital Space Station. As she was trotting along merrily, her j-phone began to Fox-a-ling-a-ling. "Of all the nerve," thought Foxanna. It was Wolverina asking her where she was. Foxanna replied, "None of your business. I am busy!"

RAWR

When she finally approached the picnic table with her purse there, she noticed another. It was her rival Wolverina's purse! "Oh Good," she said to herself as she burst out laughing. "I can snoop through it and see what is inside. She's a birdbrain - so forgetful." Then, rummaging through it thoroughly, Foxanna decided to hide it in her car. All the while, the prickly bully monsters were thrashing about wildly and sharpening up their grabster bully clawlings!

Now, Lord Computesalot was fuming! He had heard enough! Senor Smarty Pantaloons and Lord Cyborgeon had also relayed data – the bully information which he had been waiting for. The Bully Space Force was on high alert. Lockdown!

Out of the thorny thickets, the brazen bully monsters came crashing forward from everywhere imaginable, hurling frightened Foxanna up as she was trying to run for her life! At that very moment, a voice from the cosmos of Planet Bullytron screamed to her, "You, Foxanna, are on your way up to Planet Bullytron Space Academy! Your bullying will not continue, ever again!" Now, with the bold bully monsters surrounding her, she saw sonic flashes of lights as they threw her faster than the speed of lightning – up, up, and away! Planet Bullytron was watching for her and she was destined to be reprogrammed to become a kind, honest, and decent member of society.

The next morning Wolverina woke to see her purse on the kitchen table. "Now where in the world did this come from?" she said to herself as she sipped her macha tea and ate her avocado toast. Inside her purse was a note in gold handwriting from her rival Foxanna stating, "Wolverina, I'm sorry for being a bully. I'll be away for awhile. You are a wonderful principal and I hope we can become good friends." The Bully Space Force completed its mission!

TO: Wolverina
FROM: Foxanna

The next year, Foxanna and Wolverina went on the Bamaican cruise together to celebrate their friendship.

Bamaica
Cruise

About the Author

Carolyn Royer Spencer is a lifetime resident of Norfolk, Virginia. She received her B.S. in Visual Arts and her B.S. certification in Early Childhood and Elementary Education from Old Dominion University. Carolyn taught kindergarten, Title 1 kindergarten, first, and second grades for almost thirty years in Norfolk and Virginia Beach and served as a career teacher. She is a board member of the Cape Charles Historical Society. Her hobbies include golf, travel, and charity work for the children's hospital. She believes that art can be a positive means for children who have been bullied to express their inner feelings and can help them to resolve their hurt. Her first published illustrations were in the book, "Senor Smarty Pantaloons and the Mystery of the Missing Teachers".

ABOUT THE ILLUSTRATOR

Clarissa David is a Filipino-American artist, based in Norfolk VA. She received her BFA in Kinetic Imaging from Virginia Commonwealth University with a focus on video and animation.

She loves all forms of expression; video, animation, 2D & 3D ventures, craft and concept. Her work has been showcased throughout local galleries in Brooklyn and New York, including the Hirshhorn Museum in Washington DC.

Lightning Source UK Ltd.
Milton Keynes UK
UKHW052331010420
361181UK00003B/27

9 781728 349770